Karen's Pony

Look for these and other books about Karen in the Baby-sitters Little Sister series:

1 *Karen's Witch*
2 *Karen's Roller Skates*
3 *Karen's Worst Day*
4 *Karen's Kittycat Club*
5 *Karen's School Picture*
6 *Karen's Little Sister*
7 *Karen's Birthday*
8 *Karen's Haircut*
9 *Karen's Sleepover*
#10 *Karen's Grandmothers*
#11 *Karen's Prize*
#12 *Karen's Ghost*
#13 *Karen's Surprise*
#14 *Karen's New Year*
#15 *Karen's in Love*
#16 *Karen's Goldfish*
#17 *Karen's Brothers*
#18 *Karen's Home Run*
#19 *Karen's Good-bye*
#20 *Karen's Carnival*
#21 *Karen's New Teacher*
#22 *Karen's Little Witch*
#23 *Karen's Doll*
#24 *Karen's School Trip*
#25 *Karen's Pen Pal*
#26 *Karen's Ducklings*
#27 *Karen's Big Joke*
#28 *Karen's Tea Party*
#29 *Karen's Cartwheel*
#30 *Karen's Kittens*
#31 *Karen's Bully*
#32 *Karen's Pumpkin Patch*
#33 *Karen's Secret*
#34 *Karen's Snow Day*
#35 *Karen's Doll Hospital*
#36 *Karen's New Friend*
#37 *Karen's Tuba*
#38 *Karen's Big Lie*
#39 *Karen's Wedding*
#40 *Karen's Newspaper*
#41 *Karen's School*
#42 *Karen's Pizza Party*
#43 *Karen's Toothache*
#44 *Karen's Big Weekend*
#45 *Karen's Twin*
#46 *Karen's Baby-sitter*
#47 *Karen's Kite*
#48 *Karen's Two Families*
#49 *Karen's Stepmother*
#50 *Karen's Lucky Penny*
#51 *Karen's Big Top*
#52 *Karen's Mermaid*
#53 *Karen's School Bus*
#54 *Karen's Candy*
#55 *Karen's Magician*
#56 *Karen's Ice Skates*
#57 *Karen's School Mystery*
#58 *Karen's Ski Trip*
#59 *Karen's Leprechaun*
#60 *Karen's Pony*
#61 *Karen's Tattletale*

Super Specials:

1 *Karen's Wish*
2 *Karen's Plane Trip*
3 *Karen's Mystery*
4 *Karen, Hannie, and Nancy: The Three Musketeers*
5 *Karen's Baby*
6 *Karen's Campout*

Little Sister

Karen's Pony

Ann M. Martin

Illustrations by Susan Tang

SCHOLASTIC INC.
New York Toronto London Auckland Sydney

ISBN 0-590-48305-6

12 11 10 9 8 7 6 5 4 3 2 1 5 6 7 8 9/9 0/0

Printed in the U.S.A. 40

First Scholastic printing, April 1995

The author gratefully acknowledges
Stephanie Calmenson
for her help
with this book.

1

E-I-E-I-O!

Old MacDonald had a farm. E-I-E-I-O!

And on this farm he had some gorillas. E-I-E-I-O!

I was walking down the street with my best friend, Hannie. We had been singing that song all the way home on the school bus. When we ran out of farm animals, we started on jungle animals.

"See you tomorrow, Hannie," I said.

We had reached the big house. That is where I was living for the month of April. (I have two houses. A big house and a little house. I will tell you about them later.) I opened the door and raced inside.

"E-I-E-I-O!" I called. "Anybody home?"

"I am in the kitchen," replied Nannie. Nannie is my stepgrandmother. I love her a lot.

"I am here, too," said Andrew. Andrew is my little brother. He is four going on five.

"Me, too! Me, too!" said Emily Michelle. She is my little sister. She is two and a half.

I dropped my knapsack and skipped into the kitchen singing, "E-I-E-I-O!"

"Come wash up and have a snack with us," said Nannie.

Andrew and Emily were having peanut butter on crackers and apple juice. That looked like a very good snack to me. I washed my hands, then sat down at the table with them.

"Pass the peanut butter and crackers, please," I said.

I am Karen Brewer. I am seven years old. I have blonde hair, blue eyes, and a bunch of freckles. I wear glasses, too. I even have two pairs. I have a blue pair for reading. I have a pink pair for the rest of the time.

"Hello, hello! Anybody home?" called a voice.

"We are in the kitchen!" I replied.

The door opened and Kristy came in. Kristy is my stepsister. She is thirteen and the best stepsister ever.

"Mmm, looks good," said Kristy. She joined Andrew, Emily, and me.

Then David Michael marched into the kitchen. He is my stepbrother. He is seven, like me.

"Pull up a chair," said Nannie.

Sam and Charlie walked in next. They are my other stepbrothers. They are so old they are in high school. But they are not too old for an afternoon snack.

"How is everyone?" asked Charlie, between bites of peanut butter and crackers.

Daddy and Elizabeth were the last ones to come home. (Elizabeth is my very nice stepmother.)

"May we join the peanut butter party?" asked Daddy, even though it was almost dinnertime.

I looked around at my big-house family and started giggling.

"We are like Old MacDonald's Farm," I said. "Only he had lots of animals. And we have lots of people."

Ring, ring.

"I will get it," I said. I picked up the phone. But I did not say "hello." I said, "E-I-E-I-O!"

Luckily it was Mommy. She wanted to say hi to me and Andrew. She was calling us from the little house.

Andrew and I live at the big house one month. Then we switch and live at the little house. Do you want to know why? I will tell you the story.

2

A Story of Two Houses

Once upon a time, when I was really little, I lived in one big house in Stoneybrook, Connecticut, with Mommy, Daddy, and Andrew. Then Mommy and Daddy started to fight a lot. They tried their best to get along. But they just could not do it. Mommy and Daddy told Andrew and me that they loved us very much. But they did not love each other anymore. So they got divorced.

Mommy moved with Andrew and me to a little house that was not too far away. Not long after the divorce, Mommy met a nice man named Seth. Seth and Mommy got married. So now Seth is my stepfather. He lives at the little house, too. There are also some pets at the little house. They are Rocky, Seth's cat; Midgie, Seth's dog; Emily Junior, my pet rat (I named her after Emily Michelle); and Bob, Andrew's hermit crab.

After the divorce, Daddy stayed at the big house. (It is the house he grew up in.) He met someone new after the divorce, too. The person he met is Elizabeth. Elizabeth and Daddy got married. That is how Elizabeth got to be my stepmother. Elizabeth had been married before. Her children are my stepbrothers and stepsister. You already know about them. They are David Michael, Kristy, Sam, and Charlie.

And you know about my little sister, Emily Michelle. But I did not tell you yet that she was adopted. She came from a faraway country called Vietnam.

Nannie is Elizabeth's mother. She moved into the big house when Emily did. She helps take care of Emily and everyone else, too.

Now I will tell you about the pets who live at the big house. They are Shannon, David Michael's Bernese mountain dog puppy; Boo-Boo, Daddy's cranky old cat; Crystal Light the Second, my goldfish; and Goldfishie, Andrew's hippopotamus. (Just kidding! Goldfishie is a you-know-what.) Oh, I almost forgot. Emily Junior and Bob live at the big house whenever Andrew and I live there.

I have a special name for Andrew and me. I call us Andrew Two-Two and Karen Two-Two. (I got that name from a book my teacher read to our class called, *Jacob Two-Two Meets the Hooded Fang*.) Andrew and I are two-twos because we have two of so many things. We have two houses and two families, two mommies and two daddies, two cats and two dogs. We have two sets of clothes and books and toys, one at each house. I have two stuffed cats. (Goosie is my little-house cat. Moosie is my big-house cat.) I have two pieces of Tickly, my special blanket. And I have two best friends. Hannie Papadakis lives across the street from the big house. Nancy Dawes lives next door to the little house. (We call ourselves the Three Musketeers.)

It helps a lot to have two sets of things. That way Andrew and I do not have to carry so much back and forth when we switch houses each month.

Now you know the story of my two houses.

3

Family Day

I woke up on Saturday morning with the sun shining through my window. There were no April showers in sight.

"This is good news," I said to Moosie. "There is a lot I want to do today."

I wanted to roller skate with Hannie, fly my kite with Andrew, bake cupcakes with Nannie, and ride my bike with Kristy.

"I better get started, Moosie," I said.

I quickly got dressed and ran downstairs to have breakfast. Everyone was up and talking about their plans for the day.

"Ahem, ahem," said Daddy. "Your attention, please."

We stopped talking and turned to look at Daddy.

"Elizabeth and I are going to drive to an estate sale this morning. We would like all of you to come with us," he said.

"No!!!" we cried together.

Daddy and Elizabeth love estate sales. They go all the time. But we kids think they are boring.

"We have not been on an outing together in ages," said Daddy.

"We can go another day. A rainy, soggy day," I said.

"Today is a beautiful day for a drive," said Daddy. "In fact I now declare today Family Day."

That did it. We groaned. But finally we agreed to go. We could see the day was really important to Daddy. The last Family Day we had was gigundoly fun. Maybe this day would turn out to be fun, too.

We took turns calling our friends on the phone to cancel our plans. I told Nancy about the estate sale.

"Hey, do you want to come along? I could ask Daddy," I said.

"No way," Nancy replied. I did not blame her one bit.

After we made our phone calls, we piled into the van and buckled up. We were on our way.

Going to an estate sale can take a very long time. So we said sad good-byes to our Stoneybrook streets.

"Boo-hoo-hoo, good-bye!" I said. "I will probably be old and gray by the time I get back."

"I will have a beard down to my toes like Rip Van Winkle," said Sam.

"The kids I baby-sit for will be grown up by the time I come back home," said Kristy.

Then we started singing and telling jokes in the backseats. Before we knew it our

Stoneybrook streets had disappeared. We were in the countryside.

It seemed as if we drove forever. Then Daddy said, "According to the notice in the paper, this should be our turn here."

He swung the van onto a back road with a SALE sign tacked up to a tree. There were more signs with big arrows pointing to an old, run-down house. The road was not paved, so it was pretty bumpy.

"Whee!" cried Emily as she bounced up and down in her car seat.

"Oh, my. This cannot be the right place," said Elizabeth.

"I think you are right. This looks like a farm that is going out of business," said Daddy, stopping the van. "I guess we better turn around."

"No, wait! This looks like a great sale," I said.

The grown-ups were not too sure about the sale. But the kids liked it. We started

SALE
Macdonnell

piling out of the van before Daddy could change our minds.

There was neat stuff for sale everywhere we looked. There were even animals. We hurried off to start exploring.

This Family Day was going to be all right after all.

4

The Sale

I looked at the name on the mailbox and blinked twice. For a minute I thought I was on Old MacDonald's farm. But I looked again saw the name was Macdonell, not MacDonald.

The Macdonells' farm had animals, but not too many. I saw a goat, three droopy chickens, and a tired pony standing in a fenced-off area.

"Emmy go riding," said Emily.

"I do not think so," said Sam. "That pony

is too old and tired to give anyone a ride. He's a mangy thing."

Sam went off to look at a table with radios and clocks on it. Kristy went to look in some shoeboxes filled with old watches.

Soon my whole family was walking around looking at the things for sale. But I did not feel like shopping. I was too busy worrying about the poor animals on the farm. I leaned against a fence and watched them for awhile.

Then I heard something interesting. Very interesting. A man and woman were offering to buy the goat and the chickens. They talked with Mr. and Mrs. Macdonell until they agreed on a price they all thought was fair.

"We have our van out back," said the man. "We can drive the animals to our farm if you would help us load them up."

"I will have them in your van in no time," said Mr. Macdonell.

He rounded up the goat and the chickens and shooed them into the van. That left just

the pony. The poor old pony. Now he was all alone.

As the van was pulling out of the yard, I heard Mr. Macdonell say to Mrs. Macdonell, "I wish we could sell the pony, too. If no one buys him, we will have to take him to the shelter."

"Daddy! Daddy would you come here, please?" I called.

"What is it, Karen?" asked Daddy.

I explained to him about the pony. I explained how he was alone now.

"And if no one buys him, he will have to go to the shelter," I said.

"Hmm," said Daddy. "That would be too bad."

I could see Daddy was thinking hard about the pony. I decided to leave him alone and not pester him. I joined my brothers and sisters. They were still poking through the junk in the yard.

"Look at these cups," said Kristy. "There must be a hundred, and not one of them matches."

"How about this ring," said Charlie. "It would be very cool to wear a ring like this to school."

He held up a silver ring with a fancy design and a big purple stone in the center. It looked like an ancient crown from some exotic place.

"Can I hold it?" I asked. Charlie passed me the ring. As soon as I took it, the top popped open.

"Wow, neat!" I said. "It has a secret compartment. This would be a perfect place to keep my favorite fortune-cookie fortunes."

"Can I see it?" asked Kristy. "I have never seen a ring like it before."

My brothers and sisters gathered around to look at the ring. We passed it from hand to hand. Then Elizabeth came out. (She had been exploring inside the farmhouse.) We showed the ring to her.

"You kids have been such good sports about this day," she said. "If you agree to share the ring, I will buy it for you."

"All right!" we shouted. We told Elizabeth we would definitely take turns wearing it.

While Elizabeth paid for the ring, I went to look for Daddy.

5

Blueberry

Daddy was still standing by the pony. He and Mr. Macdonell were having a big conversation. I wondered what they were talking about.

I crept closer to them. I heard Daddy ask, "May I make a quick phone call?"

"Sure," replied Mr. Macdonell. He walked Daddy to the house.

"I will be right back," Daddy called to me.

While I waited for Daddy to return, I

watched the pony. He was eating hay and using his tail to swat flies off his back.

I watched until Daddy came out of the house. He hurried over to me with a big smile on his face.

"Well, Karen," he said. "It looks like you have a pony."

"I do? Oh, Daddy, thank you! Thank you so much!" I said.

"I could not bear to see that pony go to the shelter," said Daddy. "So I called my friend, Joe Cooper. Joe has a big farm. He says he has plenty of room to board a pony. So I went ahead and bought Blueberry."

"Blueberry?" I asked. "Is that my pony's name?"

"That is the name the Macdonells gave him. I figured if you liked the name, we would keep it," said Daddy.

"I love it. It is a perfect pony name," I replied.

I could hardly wait to get home to call Hannie and Nancy. I had a pony. My very own pony. I did not care if he was too old and tired to ride. I did not care if my brothers and sisters thought he was mangy. I loved him anyway. And it was a gigundoly good thing that we saved him from the shelter.

I saw the rest of my family standing by the table with the ring. I wanted to tell them the news. But I decided it was more important to wait with Daddy and Blueberry. The truck that was going to take Blueberry to Mr. Cooper's farm was already on its way.

Soon the others came over. Charlie was wearing the ring. He was waving it around for me to see.

"We could not find you. So we went ahead and drew straws to see who would wear the ring first. I won," said Charlie.

That seemed fair since Charlie found the ring in the first place.

"I was here with my pony. His name is Blueberry," I said proudly.

"Did you really buy the pony, Watson?" asked Elizabeth.

"Yes, I did," replied Daddy. "He needed to be saved from the shelter. And Joe Cooper will board him on his farm."

Just then, Blueberry threw back his head and whinnied.

"That is right, Blueberry. You do not have to worry about going to the shelter anymore," I said. "You are my pony now."

Blueberry whinnied again. I could see the news made him very happy.

We waited together until the truck came to take Blueberry to his new home.

6

The Coopers' Farm

Hannie and Nancy were very excited when I told them I owned a real, live pony. They both wanted to meet him. Daddy was taking me to see Blueberry in the morning. So I asked him if my friends could come along.

"That would be fine," said Daddy. "We can spend the day there."

Nancy's parents dropped her off early Sunday morning. Then Hannie ran across the street, and we all drove out to the Coopers' farm. This time I was happy to be waving good-bye to the Stoneybrook streets. I was happy to be going to the country to see my pony.

We drove for about half an hour. Then we turned off the highway onto a smooth road that led to the Coopers' farm. It was beautiful. Everything looked as if it had a fresh coat of paint on it. The grass and trees and flowers were bright. Even they looked freshly painted.

It was a big farm, too, with plenty of room to run in. Two big dogs and a long-haired cat came out to greet us.

"Welcome, everyone, welcome!" called Mr. Cooper.

"We are so glad to see you," said Mrs. Cooper.

I had not met the Coopers before. I was a little surprised they were so old. They looked about as old as my grandparents.

"Would you like to come inside and have some pie?" asked Mrs. Cooper.

"Thank you. But we would really like to visit my pony, if that is okay," I said.

"Of course," said Mr. Cooper. "You girls run along. Your pony is on the other side of the barn."

Hannie, Nancy, and I raced off to find Blueberry. He was in a pasture with some other horses. I could see he had not made friends with them yet. He was standing by the fence all alone.

"Here we are, Blueberry! We came to visit you," I called. Blueberry lifted his head and whinnied.

"Oh, look. He is saying hello to you," said Nancy.

"Maybe he is an old pony, but he is very sweet," said Hannie.

"Come closer, Blueberry. I have some carrots for you to eat," I said.

Nannie had given me carrots before I left. She had shown me how to hold them in the palm of my hand, so my fingers would not get nipped by mistake.

Blueberry gobbled up three carrots and nudged me for more. When the other horses saw me feeding Blueberry, they trotted over to us. As soon as they did, Blueberry walked away.

"Can we go exploring?" asked Hannie. "This farm looks like a neat place."

"That is a good idea. We should know everything about Blueberry's new home," I said. I waved to Blueberry. "We will be back soon," I told him.

We walked from one end of the farm to the other. First we peeked into the big red barn. We saw buckets of oats and bales of hay there.

In another building were cows. A farmhand named Gus introduced himself. He was milking the cows. Only he wasn't using his hands. He was using machines. He gave us each a small cup of milk to taste. I had never tried milk straight out of a cow before. It was warm and sweet.

We thanked Gus and kept walking. We passed a fenced-in area with goats, and another area with chickens. There was even a pond with ducks.

"Quack! Quack!" I called. The ducks quacked back.

We swung around and reached the farmhouse just in time to have lunch with Daddy and the Coopers. Then we went back to Blueberry to keep him company.

The minute Blueberry saw us coming, he lifted his head and whinnied just like before. When it was time for us to go, he looked sad. I hated to leave him there.

"Do not worry. I will come see you again soon," I said.

7

Emergency!

The next afternoon started out to be a lot of fun. After school Kristy was in charge of Emily, Andrew, David Michael, and me. She was supposed to watch us until five-fifteen. That was when Nannie would come home from her bowling team meeting and Charlie would come home from baseball practice.

In case you did not know it, Kristy is an excellent baby-sitter. She is even the president of a baby-sitters club she runs with her friends. They take care of kids in the neighborhood. Everyone loves them.

"Who wants popcorn and lemonade for a snack?" asked Kristy.

"Me!" we all replied.

The popcorn was easy to make because it was the microwave kind. But we decided to make the lemonade from scratch.

It was Kristy's job to cut the lemons. The rest of us took turns squeezing the lemons into a big pitcher. (We have a juicer at the big house. But it was broken.) When the lemons had been squeezed, Kristy added the water and sugar. She stirred it up and poured some into a cup.

"Sugar taster!" she called. That was my job.

I took a sip of the lemonade. Ewee! It was sour. I could feel my mouth puckering up.

"More sugar! More sugar!" I cried.

Kristy kept adding sugar. I kept tasting till the lemonade was just right.

"Hey, everyone," I said. "I have a riddle for you. What do you get when you cross a cat with a lemon?"

No one knew the answer, so I told them. "A sour puss!"

"Meow!" said Emily.

"Ha, ha," said David Michael.

Andrew was the only one besides me who thought that it was a very funny riddle.

After our snack we played Go Fish. A little before five o'clock Kristy started looking at her watch.

"I hope Charlie comes home when he promised," she said. "He is supposed to drive me to my Baby-sitters Club meeting. It starts at five-thirty and I do not want to be late."

At five minutes after five, Nannie walked in. It was a good thing, too. Right away, the phone rang. We could tell from the sound of her voice that it was emergency news.

"That was the coach from the high school," said Nannie when she hung up. "Charlie broke his hand during baseball practice. He was taken to the hospital emergency room. I am going over there right now. Kristy, you will have to stay in charge here. I am afraid that means you will miss your meeting."

"That is okay," Kristy replied. "I am just sorry Charlie is hurt."

We were all sorry Charlie was hurt. We hoped he would be okay.

8

Nurse Karen

Daddy called us from the hospital. He and Elizabeth got there right after Nannie did. Sam was there, too.

"The doctor is putting on the cast now," said Daddy. "We should be home in a couple of hours."

I wondered if Dr. Humphrey was taking care of Charlie. He took very good care of me when I broke my wrist. I broke it when I fell down roller skating. So I know everything about broken bones.

We ate peanut butter and jelly sandwiches for dinner. Then we watched TV and waited for Charlie and the rest of our family to come home. I was the first one to hear the cars pull into the driveway.

"They are here! They are here!" I shouted.

Charlie walked in with his hand in a cast and his arm in a sling.

"Ooh, Charlie, are you okay?"

"Does it hurt a lot?"

"How did it happen?"

We were all asking questions at once. Charlie told us the whole story.

"I was running for a fly ball when I tripped and fell," said Charlie. "My hand must have been twisted when I landed on it. It hurt a lot then. But it does not hurt much anymore."

"Did Dr. Humphrey put on your cast? He put my cast on when I broke my wrist," I said. I wanted to remind everyone that I had broken something, too.

"Yes, Dr. Humphrey put on my cast. He said to say hello to you," replied Charlie.

Nannie made Charlie something to eat. Then Charlie settled down to watch TV. I decided he needed a nurse to take care of him. Guess who I thought would make the best nurse. Me!

"I will get you more pillows," I said. "I think your hand will feel better if you sit up tall."

I fluffed up two pillows behind Charlie's back.

"How is that?" I asked.

"Excellent," said Charlie. "Thank you."

"You need to have your temperature taken now," I said.

"Charlie's hand is broken," said Sam. "That does not mean he is sick."

"That is right," said Charlie. "I do not need to have my temperature taken."

"Your cheeks look very red to me," I said. "I am the nurse and I am going to take your temperature."

I could not find the thermometer. So I used a straw instead. I made Charlie put the straw under his tongue and hold it there for one whole minute.

"Um, Charlie, what happened to our ring?" asked Kristy. "I do not see it on your finger. Did you leave it at the hospital?"

Charlie took the ring out of his shirt pocket and handed it to Kristy. (He could not talk because the straw was in his mouth.) Kristy put the ring on her finger.

"Time is up!" I said. I took the straw out of Charlie's mouth and studied it. "Tsk, tsk. Your temperature is nine and a half. It is time for you to go to bed."

"But I want to watch TV," said Charlie.

"You need to rest so your bones will grow back together strong," I said. "Trust me. I am your nurse."

I dragged Charlie off the couch and led him up to his room.

"If you need anything, just call," I said. I closed the door to his room.

"I need a new nurse!" called Charlie.

"I am sorry," I said. "I have been assigned to your case. I will not quit until you are better."

"Oh, all right," said Charlie. "I guess I am a little tired. Good night, Karen."

"Good night, Charlie," I said.

See what a good nurse I am?

9

Lonely

I did not get to see Blueberry on Tuesday. But on Wednesday after school, Nannie drove Andrew, David Michael, Emily, and me to the farm for a visit.

The Pink Clinker pulled into the Coopers' driveway. (The Pink Clinker is the name of Nannie's car.) I could see Blueberry out in the pasture. He looked kind of droopy. He was standing near the fence away from the other horses. I guess he had not made friends with them yet.

When Nannie stopped the car, I jumped out and ran to my pony. Andrew, David Michael, and Emily were right behind me.

Blueberry perked up as soon as he saw us. He threw back his head and whinnied.

"Hi, Blueberry!" I said.

He nudged me with his nose.

"Yes, we brought you some carrots," I told him.

Andrew, David Michael, and I took turns feeding the carrots to Blueberry. (Nannie had taken Emily into the house to visit with the Coopers.)

"What have you been up to since Sunday?" I asked.

Blueberry made a couple of loud horse noises.

"Not too much, huh? Why don't you try making friends with the other horses?" I said. "They look very nice."

Blueberry did not look interested in the

other horses. I could tell he wanted to visit with us.

"Come on, Blueberry. Let's go!" I called.

I ran alongside the fence. Blueberry followed me. David Michael and Andrew joined the line. We ran halfway around the pasture. Then we ran back again. Blueberry kept up with us the whole way. I was glad my pony was getting some exercise. He looked as if he were having fun.

I wondered who played with Blueberry when I was not there. I decided to ask someone. I went to the barn to find Gus.

"Hi, Gus," I said. "Could you please tell me who plays with Blueberry when I am not around?"

"I am afraid no one does," replied Gus. "We are all too busy with our chores. We feed Blueberry, muck out his stall, and let him loose in the pasture. That is about all we have time for."

"Oh, okay. Thanks," I said.

Poor Blueberry. It was no wonder he had looked droopy before. He was a horse who needed human company. And he was not getting any. Blueberry was just plain lonely.

10

Kristy Is Sick

When we returned home, Sam said, "I think you better come upstairs, Nannie. Kristy is sick."

I followed Nannie and Sam up to Kristy's room. Kristy was lying on her bed. She looked pale. And she was shivering.

"Nannie," said Kristy, "I do not feel very well. And there is a meeting of the Baby-sitters Club in an hour. I really want to go because I missed the last one."

"This is no time to be thinking about meetings," said Nannie. "We have to think about getting you well. Tell me what hurts you."

"I have a terrible sore throat. And I ache all over," Kristy replied.

"I will take your temperature," said Nannie. "Then we will decide what to do next."

I hoped Nannie could find the real thermometer. I did not think the straw would work too well for Kristy.

Nannie told me to wait outside Kristy's room. She did not want me to catch whatever Kristy had. She found the thermometer and put it under Kristy's tongue. When she took it out and looked at it, Nannie whistled.

"Your temperature is a hundred and two," said Nannie. "I will call the doctor and let her know we are coming. Sam, please stay here and watch the kids till your mother and Watson come home."

That meant peanut butter and jelly for dinner again.

A couple of hours later Nannie and Kristy came home.

"What did the doctor say? Are you really, really sick?" I asked.

"The doctor did a strep test on Kristy. Kristy has a raging case of strep throat," said Nannie. "She has to start taking antibiotics. And she has to stay in bed for at least a few days."

Kristy looked gloomy. "This is the second meeting in a row I have missed," she said.

"I am sure your friends understand," said Elizabeth. "If you are feeling better later, you can talk to them on the phone."

"I do not think Kristy should talk on the phone tonight," I said. "She needs her rest."

Nurse Karen was back on duty.

"Kristy, if you are going to be stuck in bed anyway, can I have my turn wearing the ring?" asked David Michael.

"It is okay with me," said Kristy. She took off the ring and handed it to David Michael.

The ring had an opening at the back, and

could be made bigger or smaller by squeezing it or pulling it apart. David Michael squeezed it a little to make it smaller, so it would not fall off his finger.

Nannie brought Kristy a tray with soup, juice, and toast. When Kristy finished eating, Nurse Karen took over.

"I want you to wear this mask and these gloves so you do not get sick, too," said Daddy.

He gave me a small white mask to cover my mouth and nose, and a pair of plastic gloves. (I had seen him wearing these things in his workshop.) When I put them on, I felt like an important surgeon ready to operate.

"Is it time for Kristy to take her medicine?" I asked.

"Yes, it is," said Elizabeth. "Thank you for reminding us."

Elizabeth brought in two pills and a cup of water.

"Just throw your head back and swallow," I said.

"Thank you, Karen. But I know how to swallow pills," Kristy replied.

Kristy sounded a little bit cranky. But that was okay. Nurses understand those things. I put a big smile on my face and got Kristy another blanket.

11

Maggie

On Saturday, Daddy dropped me off at the Coopers' farm. I was going to stay there by myself for a couple of hours.

"You do not have to worry about Karen," Mr. Cooper said to Daddy. "We will be here if she needs us."

"Maggie has offered to show Karen around the stable. Maggie is the young woman who helps out with the horses on weekends," said Mrs. Cooper.

I waved good-bye to Daddy, then followed Mrs. Cooper to the stable.

Maggie was raking out Blueberry's stall. (Blueberry was out in the pasture. I had already said hello to him.)

"Hi, Karen," said Maggie. "Are you going to help me take care of the horses today?"

I liked Maggie right away. She was like a grown-up Kristy.

"Yes," I replied. "Blueberry is my very own pony, you know."

"He is awfully sweet," said Maggie. "I just finished cleaning out his stall. But he still needs to be fed and groomed."

Lucky me. I had come just in time for the best parts.

"What will we feed Blueberry?" I asked. "I know he likes carrots."

"Yes, carrots are a treat for him. So are sliced apples and sugar cubes. But he would have to eat a lot of those things to get full. Ponies need to eat grass and hay."

I helped Maggie put some hay on a wooden frame called a rack. Then we called Blueberry in from the pasture.

"It is lunchtime, Blueberry!" I said.

I held the rope and led him into his stall.

"Remember that you must never get too close to the back of a horse. Horses are very big and strong. If a horse kicks for any reason and you are behind him, you could be hurt badly," said Maggie.

I stood off to the side and watched Blueberry eat his hay. He finished every bit. Then he drank from a bucket of fresh water.

"I guess Blueberry was hungry," I said.

"Horses are big animals. They need a lot of food," said Maggie. "But they cannot eat too much at one time because their stomachs are small for their bodies. That is why we feed them at least three times a day."

"Is it time to groom him now?" I asked. "Can we braid his hair and put ribbons in it?"

"I am sure he would look very nice with ribbons and braids," replied Maggie. "But we do not have time to do anything fancy today. We will just make sure his coat is neat and healthy."

Maggie carried over a box that was filled to the top with all kinds of brushes and things.

"Even my dolls do not have so many brushes and combs," I said.

"Each brush, comb, and pick has a special job," said Maggie. "Here is what we will do. First we will use the currycomb. That will clean up his coat."

She held up an oval brush that was made of rubber.

"Next we will use a softer brush to make his coat nice and smooth. Then we will comb his mane and tail. The last thing we will do is wipe him down with a cloth," said Maggie. "You will see how great Blueberry can look."

I started with the currycomb. I could see the dead hairs flying off Blueberry. Then Maggie showed me how to use long strokes with the soft brush. Blueberry's coat started to glow.

"This is my favorite part of taking care

of Blueberry," I said to Maggie. "I can tell he really likes it."

We combed Blueberry's mane and tail. Then we each took a soft cloth and wiped him down.

I stepped back to admire our work. No one could call my pony mangy now. Blueberry looked beautiful!

12

Roddie

"Could we go to the farm again, Daddy? Could we, please?" I asked. It was Sunday. I wanted to spend more time with Blueberry.

"Have you finished all your homework?" asked Daddy.

"Yes, I have," I replied.

"Come on, then. I will drop you off and you can visit for a couple of hours," said Daddy.

As soon as I got to the pasture, Blueberry raised his head and whinnied just like always. Maggie was busy grooming one of the other horses. We waved hello to each other.

I decided it was time to have a talk with Blueberry. He was spending too much time by himself.

"Blueberry," I said, "tomorrow is Monday. I do not think I will be able to visit you. I want you to try hard to make friends with the other horses. You will be much happier if you play with them."

Blueberry made some horse noises and turned his head away. I do not think he liked my idea.

"Come on, Blueberry. It makes me sad when you are all alone and droopy," I said.

Just then Blueberry raised his head and whinnied again. A boy was walking toward us. He looked about my age.

"Hi. My name is Roddie Gale," said the boy. "Who are you?"

"I am Karen," I replied.

"My parents just bought the farm down

the road," said Roddie. "I guess that makes us neighbors."

"I do not live here. I live in Stoneybrook," I said. "This is my pony, Blueberry. He lives here and I come to visit him whenever I can."

"He looks like a nice pony," said Roddie. "Is it okay if I pet him?"

"Sure," I replied. "He does not like other horses so much. But he really likes people."

I watched Roddie pet Blueberry. He and Blueberry seemed to like each other.

"I have some carrots. You can feed Blueberry if you want to," I said.

Roddie held the carrots out in the palm of his hand just the way he was supposed to.

"You are lucky you have a pony. I wish I could have one," said Roddie.

"Why can't you?" I asked.

"My parents have a rule that any animal who lives on our farm has to earn its keep. We have chickens because they lay eggs

And we have a goat and a cow because they give us milk. But a horse could not give us any food. And it costs a lot of money to keep a horse."

"Maybe the horse could pull a wagon or something," I said.

"That is a good idea. But it would not help us. We do not have a wagon. My mom and dad are not farmers. My dad works in an office in Stoneybrook. My mom is a librarian," said Roddie. "They just like living on a farm."

"Well, you can visit Blueberry as much as you want," I said. "No one around here has time to play with him. He gets very lonely. I would like him to have company."

"I do not have too much free time. After school I have a lot of chores to do," said Roddie. "But I promise I will visit him whenever I can."

Roddie was nice. We played with Blueberry for a while. Then I showed him around the farm. By the time we got back to the Coopers' house, Daddy was waiting to take me home.

"I have to go now," I said. "Will you really come visit Blueberry?"

"I promise," replied Roddie.

Roddie headed back down the road to his farm. I got into the car with Daddy. As we drove away, I could see Blueberry looking droopy and sad again. I hoped Roddie would visit him soon.

13

Ouch! Ouch!

When I got home, Andrew and David Michael were in the yard with Melody and Bill Korman. (Melody is seven. Bill is nine. They live just down the street from the big house.) Then Hannie called and asked if she could come over.

"Sure," I replied. "Bring Linny, too." (Linny is Hannie's brother. He is David Michael's friend.)

That made seven kids altogether.

"Who wants to play freeze tag?" I asked.

Everyone thought that was a great idea. Linny got to be "It" first.

I love to play freeze tag. First of all, I am very good at not being tagged. But even if I do get tagged, I always get frozen in a funny position.

"On your mark, get set, go!" called Linny.

I ran to the left. I ran to the right. I swung around one tree. Then another. I passed David Michael and waved. He was running in the opposite direction and waved back. Then down he went.

"Ouch! Ouch!" cried David Michael.

"Time out!" I shouted.

I ran to David Michael to see if he was okay. He was not.

"Ooh, my elbow. It hurts. It hurts. It got twisted when I fell." David Michael moaned.

I ran inside the house to get help. Daddy, Elizabeth, and Nannie came running outside.

"You will be fine," said Daddy. "But I

can see your elbow is swelling up. You may have dislocated it."

Elizabeth was already starting the station wagon. Daddy carried David Michael to the car and buckled him up in the backseat.

"We will call you from the hospital," said Elizabeth.

"This family is becoming awfully familiar with the Stoneybrook medical facilities," said Nannie.

My friends and I waved good-bye as the car pulled out of the driveway. No one felt much like playing anymore. So everyone went home.

I waited downstairs with Andrew, Emily, and Nannie for Elizabeth to call. (Kristy and Charlie were resting in their rooms upstairs. Sam was out with his friends.) We waited and waited. Finally the phone rang. Nannie answered it. When she hung up, she did not look too happy.

"Your father was right. David Michael dislocated his elbow," said Nannie.

"That is too bad," I said.

I had to work fast. This was another job for Nurse Karen. I ran upstairs to get ready.

By the time David Michael came home, I was dressed in white. I had even made myself a white nurse's cap. My knapsack was filled with important medical supplies. Straw thermometer. Bandages. Funny books to read. Dolls for company. Candy to eat.

Kristy and Charlie were both feeling much better. That meant I could turn my full attention to my latest case — David Michael's dislocated elbow.

"I need to take your temperature," I said to my brother.

"They already did that at the hospital. I do not have a temperature," said David Michael.

"I think we need to take it again," I said.

"No way," said David Michael. He shut his mouth tightly.

No problem. I had discovered a few

scratches on his right hand. I decided some bandages would help.

"Your hand needs more treatment," I said. "And, um, do you think it is my turn to wear the ring yet?"

"I will give you the ring if you leave me alone," said David Michael.

That sounded like a fair deal to me. I took the ring from David Michael. Then I went back upstairs to check on my other patients.

14

Spooky!

On Sunday night, Sam called a meeting for all us kids. (Emily Michelle did not come. She is still too little for meetings.) We met in the TV room. That is where David Michael was recovering.

Sam turned off the TV, then stood up in the center of the room.

"I have made an important discovery," he said.

(That got our attention fast.)

"I have been thinking about our ring," he continued. "Look what happened to each person who wore it. First Charlie wore it and broke his hand. Then Kristy wore it and got a terrible strep throat. Then David Michael wore it and dislocated his elbow. I have decided that the ring must be bad luck."

We all gasped. Sam had to be right. There was no other explanation for the bad things happening to our family.

"Ooh, spooky!" I said. "Maybe there is an invisible evil potion in the secret compartment."

"That could be," said Kristy. "I felt funny the minute I put it on."

"Maybe it belonged to a mean magician. It has magical powers that make bad things happen to whoever wears it," said David Michael.

"I am scared of that ring. I do not want to wear it. I do not want to!" cried Andrew.

"Do not worry," said Charlie. "You do not have to wear it. We will have to decide together what to do with it."

"I think we should bury it someplace far away," said David Michael. "Or maybe we should throw it in the ocean."

"But then bad things could happen to the fish," I said. "That would be mean. I like fish."

"It is six of us against one ring. I say we have a ceremony and take away its secret powers. That way the ring will not hurt anyone ever again," said Sam.

We decided that was the best idea.

"Who has the ring now?" asked Charlie.

"I gave it to you, Karen," said David Michael. "But you are not wearing it. Where is it?"

"I must have put it upstairs," I replied. "I will be right back."

I ran to my room to get the ring. I looked on my dresser. No ring. I looked on my bed. No ring. I looked on the floor. No ring.

"Moosie," I said to my stuffed cat, "did you see the ring?"

I held Moosie up to my ear so he could tell me where it was. But Moosie had not seen it.

Uh-oh, I thought. I raced back downstairs and stood in the center of the TV room.

"I have made an important new discovery," I said. "The ring has vanished!"

15

The Search

"The ring has to be somewhere," said Kristy. "It cannot just vanish into thin air."

"Why not? It has magic powers, doesn't it?" I said.

"We cannot take any chances," said Charlie. "If it is in our house, more bad things could happen to us. We have to look for it *everywhere.*"

"I say we split up and search for it," said Sam.

"Oh, no!" I said. "Let's stick together. I

would be too scared if I found it by myself."

"Me, too," said Andrew.

"That is a good idea," said Charlie. "We will start upstairs and work our way down."

The six of us marched up to the attic. We looked and looked, but we did not find it. We searched every room on the second floor. I found a Barbie shoe I had been looking for. But we did not find the ring. We went downstairs to the first floor. It was not there either.

"Maybe we threw it out with the trash," said Sam.

"Let's go look," said Charlie.

On our way outside, Elizabeth stopped us.

"Where are you kids going?" she asked. "And David Michael, what are you doing up? You hurt yourself very badly today."

"I am okay," said David Michael. "We lost something and we have to look for it together."

Elizabeth decided not to ask any more questions.

"Please do not stay out too long," she said.

We searched in the dark through the yucky trash. But we still could not find the ring. When we got back to the TV room, we fell down in a heap. I looked at the clock. We had been searching for over an hour.

"I do not think we should worry too much anymore," said Charlie. "I am sure the ring is only bad luck if you are actually wearing it or carrying it."

"I think you are right," I said. "I remember reading that once in a book."

(I did not really remember reading it. But it sounded more official that way.)

"We can look for it again tomorrow," said Sam. "Maybe it was in the yard, but it was just too dark to see it."

"I am tired," said Kristy. "And tomorrow is my first day back in school. I am going to sleep."

We were all tired. We said good night and went to our rooms.

When I got into bed, I hugged Moosie close to me. I looked around the room one more time, to make sure the ring was not there. Then I turned out the light and closed my eyes.

I kept seeing rings floating in the air. It took me a long time to fall asleep.

16

Blueberry's Problem

The next time I saw Blueberry was the following weekend. Daddy drove me to the farm on Saturday.

When we pulled into the driveway, I was glad to see Roddie visiting Blueberry. Blueberry did not look sad and droopy. He looked happy.

"Will you come with me, Daddy? You have not visited Blueberry in a long time," I said. "I want you to meet Roddie Gale, too. He is really nice."

"Let me just say hello to Mr. and Mrs. Cooper. Then I will join you," Daddy replied.

I said hi to Blueberry and Roddie and Maggie. The Coopers' farm was starting to feel like my second home.

"This is the third time I have visited Blueberry this week," said Roddie. "You are right. He really does like people. He does not play with the other horses at all."

When Daddy came outside, I introduced him to Roddie and Maggie. Then I showed him the things I had learned.

"This is a currycomb," I said importantly. "You use it to get rid of the dead hairs. That is how to make a pony look beautiful."

"Why don't we groom Blueberry together?" said Daddy. "It looks like Maggie is busy taking care of the other horses now."

Daddy, Roddie, and I brushed Blueberry. Then we combed him. Then we wiped him down with a cloth till his coat was shining.

"This is the biggest pet you have ever had to take care of," said Daddy. "You are doing a very good job."

"Thank you," I replied.

Before we left, we made sure that Blueberry had fresh hay to eat and water to drink.

"Can we come again tomorrow?" I asked.

"Tomorrow would be fine," Daddy replied.

"I can come again tomorrow, too," said Roddie. "See you then."

Daddy and I got into the car. Roddie waved good-bye and walked across the field. The minute we were gone, Blueberry started to look droopy and look sad.

I decided it was time to talk to Daddy. I knew he was trying to do his best for Blueberry. But the Coopers' farm was just not working out.

"Daddy, I have something important to

tell you about Blueberry," I said.

"I am listening," replied Daddy.

"The Coopers' farm is very beautiful," I said. "And Mr. and Mrs. Cooper are very nice. But I do not think Blueberry likes living on their farm. He does not like to play with the other horses. And the farm hands are too busy to pay attention to him. Blueberry is really lonely. But I know someplace where he would be happy."

"Where is that?" asked Daddy.

"I think Blueberry would be happier on Roddie's farm. But there is a big problem. Roddie is not allowed to have a pony. His parents have a rule. They only have animals that earn their keep. They have chickens, a goat, and a cow. But they do not have any horses."

"Hmm," said Daddy. "I would like some time to think about this problem. I do not want Blueberry to be unhappy. Maybe there is something we can do."

"Thanks, Daddy," I said.

I kept quiet the rest of way, so Daddy could think. When we got home, he got right on the phone. He talked on the phone a long time.

17

A New Home for Blueberry

After dinner on Saturday, Daddy called me into the den for a talk.

"First of all, I am proud of you for speaking up about Blueberry's problem. I know it was not easy for you to tell me the Coopers' farm was not working out," said Daddy. "The second thing I want to tell you is that I think we have a solution to the problem."

"All right!" I said. "What is it?"

"I spoke with Roddie's parents," said

Daddy. "I arranged to board Blueberry at their farm instead of with the Coopers. The boarding money will cover Blueberry's expenses, so he will be earning his keep like the other animals. He will be in a place where he can get more attention, especially from your friend, Roddie. What do you think of the plan?"

"It is a very good plan," I said.

I was happy that Blueberry was going to a better place. But I was also a little jealous that Roddie would get to spend more time with him than I would.

"Will Roddie's parents let me visit Blueberry?" I asked.

"Of course," said Daddy. "Blueberry is still going to be your pony. You can see him often."

I decided to act grown-up about Blueberry's new home. After all, it was the perfect solution to the problem.

The next day, Daddy took me to the farm so I could be with Blueberry when he moved. A blue van was parked by the pasture.

"Hello, Mr. O'Brien," said Daddy. "I am Watson Brewer and this is my daughter, Karen. Are we ready to move Blueberry?"

"We are ready," replied Mr. O'Brien. "We were just waiting for you to arrive."

Mr. O'Brien and another man tried to lead Blueberry up a ramp and into the van. But Blueberry would not go.

"I think he is a little scared," said Mr. O'Brien.

"He is my pony," I said. "Maybe I should talk to him."

Mr. O'Brien thought that was a good idea. I whispered in Blueberry's ear. "You do not have to be scared. You are going down the road to Roddie's farm. You like Roddie. And I will still come to visit you."

I fed Blueberry a carrot. I petted him. Then I said to Mr. O'Brien, "I think we can try again."

This time Blueberry walked up the ramp. Mr. O'Brien closed the doors to the van and headed up the road to the Gales' farm. Daddy and I followed right behind.

18

The Mystery

Roddie and his parents were waiting outside when we pulled up to their house. His parents looked awfully familiar. Had I seen them somewhere before? Hmm. I could not remember from where. It was a mystery.

"Hello, Mr. and Mrs. Gale," said Daddy. "I am Watson Brewer. It is a pleasure to meet you."

Roddie introduced me to his parents. Then he gave me on a tour of his farm. First he took me to see the cow. Her name was Betsy.

"I know the Coopers use machines to milk their cows," said Roddie. "We milk Betsy by hand. I will show you how sometime if you want to learn."

Next Roddie showed me a goat. And he showed me three chickens. That is when I remembered! Mr. and Mrs. Gale were the people I had seen at the estate sale. They were the ones who had bought the goat and the chickens from the Macdonells. The mystery was solved.

This was truly the perfect place for Blueberry. He was going to be with his old pals again. I told Roddie the story of Blueberry and his friends.

"It was a sunny day and my brothers and sisters and I did *not* want to go to an estate sale. But Daddy wanted us to have a Family Day. We pulled into the Macdonells' farm by mistake. Then your parents bought the goat and the chickens and Daddy bought

Blueberry. And now they will all be together again!" I said.

"Cool!" exclaimed Roddie.

"Come on," I said. "Let's go keep Blueberry company. We have to make sure he is comfortable in his new home."

Blueberry was already chomping on some hay. Roddie's parents had fixed up a bright, clean stall for him.

"He is a very sweet pony," said Mrs. Gale. "We will be happy to have him here."

"And we will be happy to have you visit as often as you like," said Mr. Gale. "I know that Roddie has been enjoying your company."

"Is it okay if we take Blueberry for a little walk?" I asked.

"Go right ahead," said Mr. Gale. "When you finish, come in the house and have some lemonade."

"Thank you," I replied.

Roddie and I led Blueberry across the

yard to see his old friends. When he saw them, he threw back his head and whinnied.

"You are home, Blueberry," I said. "You have a real and true home and you will not have to leave."

19

The Good-Luck Ring

"I think Blueberry is going to be happy in his new home. Don't you agree?" asked Daddy.

"I sure do," I said.

We were in the car driving home from the Gales' farm. For some reason I was feeling fidgety. Something on the car seat kept jabbing me. I ran my hand across the seat. Nothing was there. I slipped my hand into the back pocket of my jeans.

Oh, boy! I found it. I found the ring. I

must have put it there when David Michael handed it to me the week before.

I quickly pulled my hand out of my pocket. I rubbed my hand on the car seat. I blew on it. I waved it in the air.

"Are you okay, Karen?" asked Daddy.

"Yes. At least I think so," I replied.

But I was not too sure. I had touched the bad-luck ring. Who could tell what would happen to me next?

Then I realized something. I had been wearing the same jeans for a couple of days. And for the last two days I had been having very good luck. Yesterday Daddy made our good plans for Blueberry. Today, we met the goat and the chickens on Roddie's farm.

Daddy always says that a person's luck can change. If a person's luck can change, a ring's luck can change too. Maybe it had stopped being a bad-luck ring. Maybe it had turned into a good-luck ring. I could hardly wait to get home. I had to call a meeting to tell my brothers and sisters the news.

The minute I got into the house, I called everyone into the TV room.

"Guess what," I said. "I found the ring!"

I held it up in the air. My brothers and sister jumped back.

"Wait," I said. "You do not have to be afraid of it. It is a good-luck ring now."

They looked at me as if I had two heads. I could see I had another long story to tell. I started by saying that I must have put the ring in my pocket when David Michael handed it to me. Then I told them about the good things that had happened to me since then.

"So you see, it really is a good-luck ring," I said.

"I am not taking any chances," said Charlie. "If you like the ring, you can have it."

"Would you like to share it with me, Kristy?" I asked.

Kristy shook her head.

"Would *anyone* like to share it with me?" I asked.

"No, thank you," said Sam. "The ring is all yours."

That sounded like one more piece of good luck for me.

20

My Beautiful Pony

The next Saturday, I invited Hannie and Nancy to visit Blueberry with me. Nannie dropped us off at Roddie's farm.

"Have a good time, girls," said Nannie. "I will come back to get you in a couple of hours."

As soon as Blueberry saw me coming, he lifted his head and whinnied. That made me happy. Blueberry may have a new home, I thought, but he is still my pony.

I introduced Hannie and Nancy to Roddie and his parents. Then Roddie and I gave my friends a tour of the farm.

"This is Betsy, Roddie's cow," I said. "Roddie promised to teach me how to milk her."

Next we found the goat and chickens.

"These are Blueberry's old pals," said Roddie.

"What are their names?" asked Nancy.

"We were thinking of naming the chickens Annie, Frannie, and Hannie," said Roddie.

"A chicken named after me? I like that!" said Hannie.

"Okay," said Roddie. "Those will be their names. We did not think of a name for the goat yet."

"Is it a boy goat, or a girl goat?" asked Nancy.

"It is a girl goat. She gives us milk for my mom to drink. My mom is allergic to cow's milk," said Roddie.

"Why don't you call her Huckleberry," I

said. "That would be a good name for Blueberry's friend."

Everyone liked that name a lot.

"Hello, Huckleberry!" I said.

Huckleberry bleated. I guess she liked her name, too.

"Can we visit Blueberry now? I want to spend as much time with him as I can," I said.

We went back to the pasture. On the way, Roddie got some sliced apples from the kitchen. We fed them to Blueberry.

We took turns brushing him. I showed Hannie and Nancy how to make him look shiny and beautiful.

We took him for a walk around the farm to see his friends. Then we went back to the pasture. Blueberry was happy eating grass, with us beside him for company.

While we were visiting with Blueberry, I made a daisy chain. I linked the daisies together stem by stem.

Beep, beep! Nannie was driving up the

road in the Pink Clinker. I got up and waved to her.

"It is time for me to go home, Blueberry," I said. "Roddie will take good care of you while I am gone."

"I sure will," said Roddie. "You do not have to worry about your pony while he is with me."

There was one more thing I wanted to do.

"I will be right there, Nannie!" I called.

I linked together the two ends of the daisy chain. I set the crown of daisies on Blueberry's head. Then I put my arms around his neck and gave him a great big hug.

"Good-bye, my beautiful pony," I said. "I will see you again soon."

About the Author

ANN M. MARTIN lives in New York City and loves animals, especially cats. She has two cats of her own, Mouse and Rosie.

Other books by Ann M. Martin that you might enjoy are *Stage Fright*; *Me and Katie (the Pest)*; and the books in *The Baby-sitters Club* series.

Ann likes ice cream and *I Love Lucy*. And she has her own little sister, whose name is Jane.

Don't miss #61

KAREN'S TATTLETALE

"Mommy, Seth — Karen did not put her napkin in her lap," said Andrew.

I jammed my napkin into my lap. Then I tried to eat a peaceful breakfast. But Andrew would not let me.

"Hey, Karen is putting sugar on her cereal," he announced.

"Karen, you know that cereal does not need sugar," said Seth. "We have been through this before. It is full of sugar already."

I put the spoon back in the sugar bowl. Then I glared at Andrew.

"Seth, Karen is staring at me," said Andrew.

"Karen, are you finished with your breakfast?" asked Seth.

"In a big way," I replied.

The Baby-sitters Little Sister titles continued...

❑	MQ44825-0	#29	Karen's Cartwheel	$2.75
❑	MQ45645-8	#30	Karen's Kittens	$2.75
❑	MQ45646-6	#31	Karen's Bully	$2.95
❑	MQ45647-4	#32	Karen's Pumpkin Patch	$2.95
❑	MQ45648-2	#33	Karen's Secret	$2.95
❑	MQ45650-4	#34	Karen's Snow Day	$2.95
❑	MQ45652-0	#35	Karen's Doll Hospital	$2.95
❑	MQ45651-2	#36	Karen's New Friend	$2.95
❑	MQ45653-9	#37	Karen's Tuba	$2.95
❑	MQ45655-5	#38	Karen's Big Lie	$2.95
❑	MQ45654-7	#39	Karen's Wedding	$2.95
❑	MQ47040-X	#40	Karen's Newspaper	$2.95
❑	MQ47041-8	#41	Karen's School	$2.95
❑	MQ47042-6	#42	Karen's Pizza Party	$2.95
❑	MQ46912-6	#43	Karen's Toothache	$2.95
❑	MQ47043-4	#44	Karen's Big Weekend	$2.95
❑	MQ47044-2	#45	Karen's Twin	$2.95
❑	MQ47045-0	#46	Karen's Baby-sitter	$2.95
❑	MQ43647-3		Karen's Wish Super Special #1	$2.95
❑	MQ44834-X		Karen's Plane Trip Super Special #2	$3.25
❑	MQ44827-7		Karen's Mystery Super Special #3	$2.95
❑	MQ45644-X		Karen's Three Musketeers Super Special #4	$2.95
❑	MQ45649-0		Karen's Baby Super Special #5	$3.25
❑	MQ46911-8		Karen's Campout Super Special #6	$3.25

Available wherever you buy books, or use this order form.

Scholastic Inc., P.O. Box 7502, 2931 E. McCarty Street, Jefferson City, MO 65102

Please send me the books I have checked above. I am enclosing $ ____________

(please add $2.00 to cover shipping and handling). Send check or money order - no cash or C.O.Ds please.

Name ______________________________ Birthdate ____________

Address ____

City ____________________ State/Zip ____________________

Please allow four to six weeks for delivery. Offer good in U.S.A. only. Sorry, mail orders are not available to residents to Canada. Prices subject to change.

BLS793